W9-BMX-727

Merry Christmas!
Sarah, Mama

How to Trick the Tooth Fairy

How to Trick the Tooth Fairy

By Erin Danielle Russell

Illustrated by Jennifer Hansen Rolli

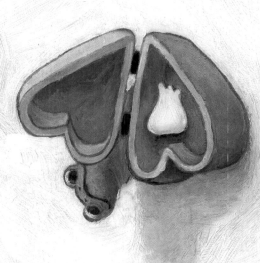

Aladdin

NEW YORK   LONDON   TORONTO   SYDNEY   NEW DELHI

ALADDIN | An imprint of Simon & Schuster Children's Publishing Division | 1230 Avenue of the Americas, New York, New York 10020 | First Aladdin hardcover edition May 2018 | Text copyright © 2018 by Erin Danielle Russell | Illustrations copyright © 2018 by Jennifer Hansen Rolli | All rights reserved, including the right of reproduction in whole or in part in any form. | ALADDIN and related logo are registered trademarks of Simon & Schuster, Inc. | For information about special discounts for bulk purchases, please contact Simon & Schuster Special Sales at 1-866-506-1949 or business@simonandschuster.com. | The Simon & Schuster Speakers Bureau can bring authors to your live event. For more information or to book an event contact the Simon & Schuster Speakers Bureau at 1-866-248-3049 or visit our website at ww.simonspeakers.com. | Book designed by Karin Paprocki | The illustrations for this book are rendered with oil paint on brown craft paper with digital enhancement. | The text of this book was set in Oneleigh. | Manufactured in China 0218 SCP | 10 9 8 7 6 5 4 3 2 1 | Library of Congress Control Number 2017955447 | ISBN 978-1-4814-6732-2 (hc) | ISBN 978-1-4814-6733-9 (eBook)

To my mom and dad for all their love, help, and encouragement.
Thank you for believing in me!

And to the Tooth Fairy for all the magical years
of dollar bills and fairy-dust cookies

—E. D. R.

To my dear sisters, Heather and Beth,
who were all too often the deliverers of tricky treats

—J. H. R.

Kaylee *loved* to pull pranks.

Prank princess
in training

Favorite holiday is
April Fool's Day

Comfy shoes
for creeping

Twinkle of
mischief

Cute as a button,
sharp as a tack

She pulled pranks every day . . . .

every night . . . .

and even on holidays.

She was *always* looking for her next unsuspecting victim.

But was Kaylee the princess of pranks?

No.

That would be this little trickster. . . .

THE TOOTH FAIRY!

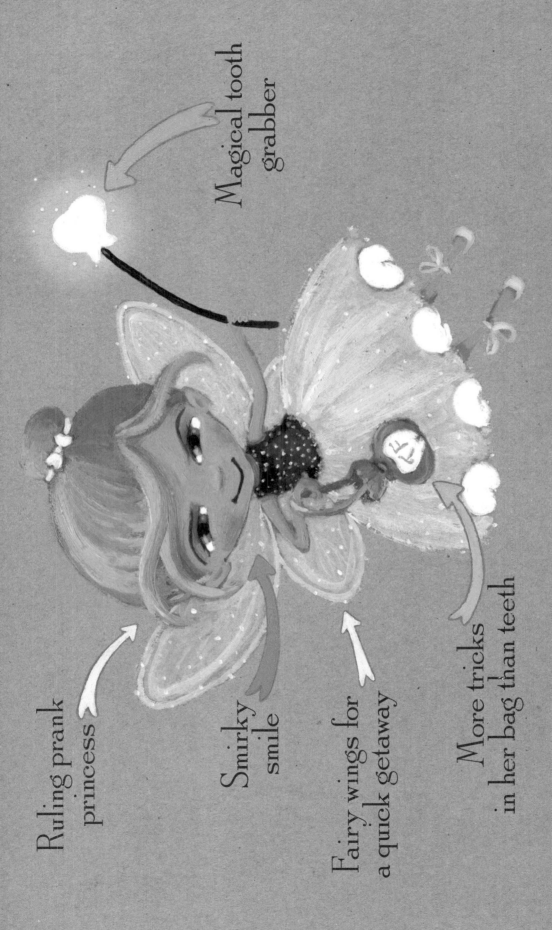

Magical tooth grabber

Ruling prank princess

Smirky smile

Fairy wings for a quick getaway

More tricks in her bag than teeth

But she had no clue whom she was about to meet . . . .

Shhhhhhhhh...

The Tooth Fairy was expecting to find something small, smooth, and white,

EEEEEEK!

not green with webbed feet!

Now, if you prank the Tooth Fairy

with a *fake* frog, you'll get . . .

REAL FROGS!

Game on!

Had Kaylee finally met
her mischief-making match?

She offered the Tooth Fairy a slice of pie.

I'm so, so, sooooooo soooooo sorry.

And if you know anything about fairies, you know they LOOOOOVE sweets.

The Tooth Fairy
dug into her dessert.
Suddenly her mouth
was on fire!

Now, if you prank
the Tooth Fairy
with prankster pie,
she'll top it with . . .

GOBS OF GOOEY
ICE CREAM!

Kaylee was a mess!

But once the sprayer was in her hands, Kaylee turned it on the Tooth Fairy!

Pass the sprayer, please.

Now, if you prank the Tooth Fairy with a splash of water, she'll make it . . .

Whoooooooooooosshhhhh

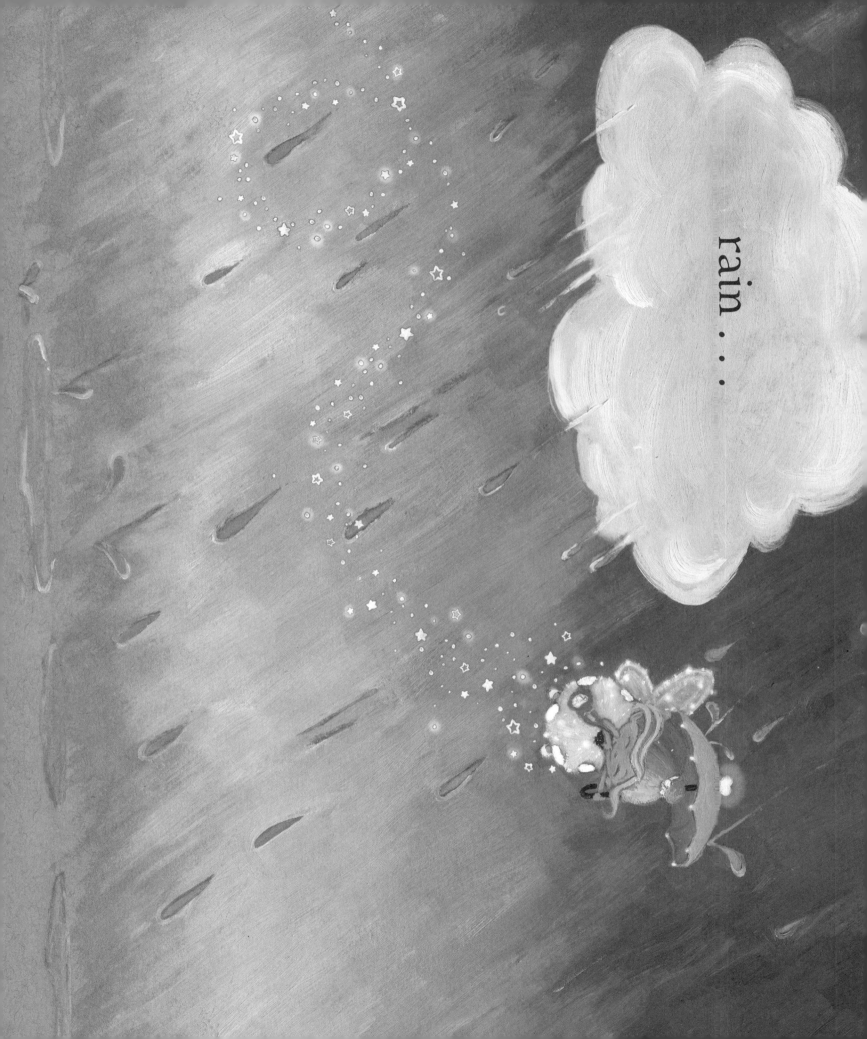

rain . . .

Storms scared Kaylee!
She ran and hid behind a closet door.

The Tooth Fairy wanted to out-prank Kaylee,
but frightening her wasn't fun at all.

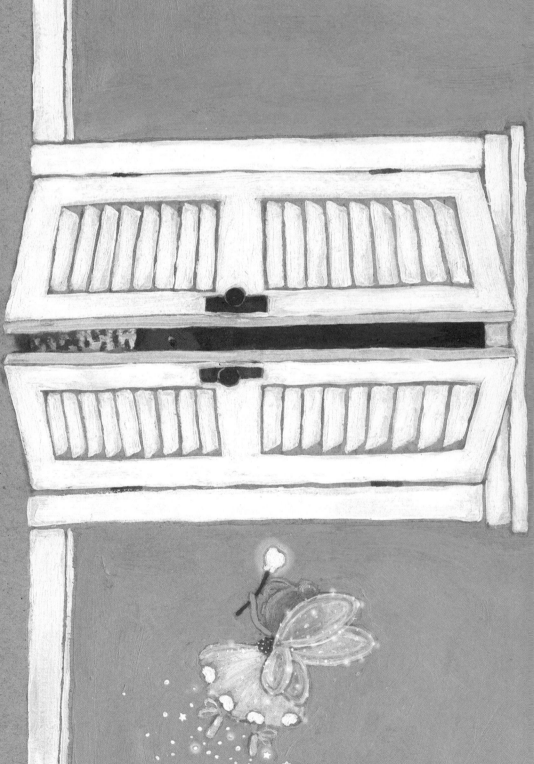

Kaylee sprang out of hiding, surprising the Tooth Fairy with a burst of bubble gum.

TOPSY-TURVY

TOOTH FAIRY TROUBLE!

Kaylee and the Tooth Fairy may have been
soaked
and scared
and stunned.

But luckily . . . .

Kaylee had one more trick
up her pajama sleeve.

And together,
they cleaned up
their mess.

And so did the
Tooth Fairy. . . .

Now, if you know
anything about pranksters
and fairies . . .

you know there's room for lots
of fairy-dust cookies,